a Rumpus in the Night

by Nick Ward

WORTHWHILE
BOOKS

Right in the middle of a scary monster dream,
Jamie woke up.

I'm coming to get you!

RARR!

He woke up so suddenly
that part of his dream stayed with him,
and crashing into his bedroom came...

a Rumpus!

It was one of the monsters
from Jamie's dream,
and the monster looked
very surprised!

"**Help!**"
roared Jamie.
"There's a monster in my room!"

"**Help!**"
cried the Rumpus in a snuffly, gruffly voice.
"There's a horrible, roaring monster pointing at me!"

Then with a clash and a clatter, the Rumpus dived under Jamie's bed.

Jamie was astonished. *Surely, hairy little monsters don't get scared*, he thought. "Come out, monster. I won't hurt you," whispered Jamie, leaning over.

The Rumpus crawled out from under the bed.
"It's dark and I'm scared and I want to go home," he whimpered.

"You're from my dream," said Jamie.
"How do you get home?"

"You have to go back to sleep,"
    snuffled the Rumpus.

"And then I'll pop back into your dream."

"But I'm wide awake now," said Jamie, turning on the light. "And if I can't go to sleep, Mom always reads me a story."

"But I can't read," said the Rumpus.

"Then I'll read you a story," Jamie said. "And maybe that will help us both fall asleep."

So the Rumpus tried to climb onto Jamie's bed.
"**Whoa!**" he cried as the covers started to slip.

Whoa!

"Quiet, Rumpus!" whispered Jamie as the monster slid to the floor with a thump. "You'll wake everyone up!"

"It's not a scary story, is it?" asked a muffled Rumpus from under a tangle of blankets and sheets. "I don't like scary stories."

Mumf!

Jamie read one story, then another, **then** the first story all over again...
but he and the Rumpus were **still** wide awake.

"Sometimes I'm allowed to play a game if I can't sleep," said Jamie.
"Let's play Chutes and Ladders."

BANG!

"Is that a **snake** on the box?" squealed the Rumpus. He jumped into the cupboard to hide, and with a crash, the nervous monster pulled down the rod of clothes.

CRASH!

OOF!

"I d-don't like s-snakes," stuttered a muffled voice from beneath a pile of coats.

"It's only a game," Jamie said. "Come out and I'll show you."

"I'M THE WINNER!" roared the Rumpus, marching around the bedroom in triumph. "Let's play again ... whoops!" He tripped over the game and sent it flying through the air.

CR

ASH!

"Shh!" said Jamie. "You'll wake everyone up!"

"Sorry," whispered the Rumpus. "Aren't you sleepy yet?"

"Not one little bit," Jamie answered with a sigh. "Let's play tag. You're it!"

"I'm what?" asked the Rumpus, not understanding the game at all.

I'm coming to get you!

Jamie laughed.
"You're the monster!
And you've got to catch me!"

The Rumpus chased after him.

"Now *you're* the monster!" he cried, tagging Jamie.

"No, *you're* the monster!"
Jamie yelled back.

Then Jamie and the Rumpus played follow-the-leader. They marched...

and jumped...

and skipped.

They bounced on Jamie's bed and made a GREAT HULLABALOO...

until they were completely worn out.
"I'm not scared anymore," panted the Rumpus, collapsing in a heap.
"Don't go to sleep yet. I want to play some more."

"But I'm so tired," said Jamie, yawning as he crawled into bed. "I'm so..."

"Wake up, Jamie!" cried the Rumpus.

But Jamie fell fast asleep, and the Rumpus...
disappeared.

Far, far away in another world,
a **Rumpus** woke up in the **middle**
of a scary monster dream.
He woke up so **suddenly**
that part of his dream stayed with him,
and **crashing** into his bedroom came . . .

Jamie!

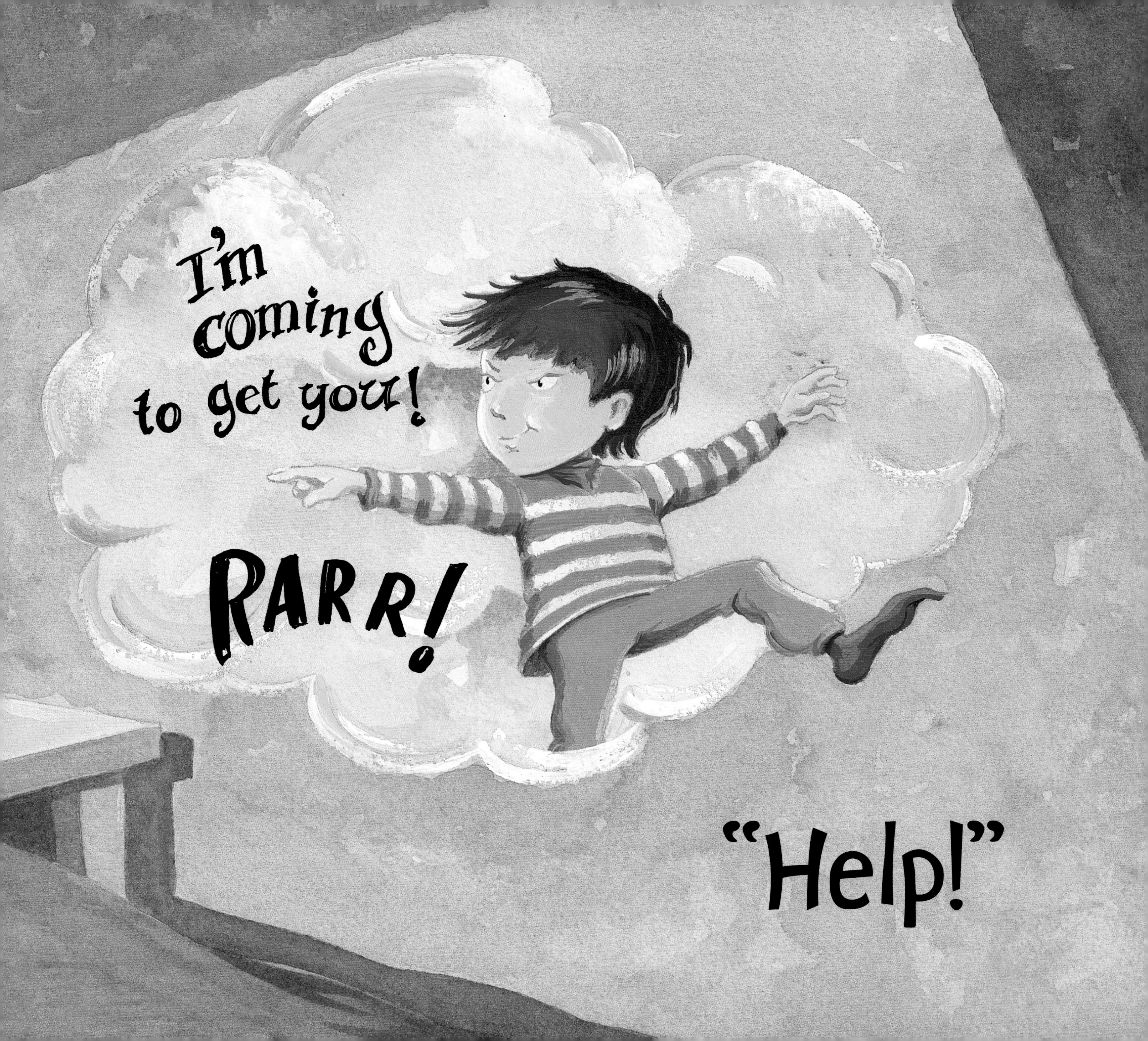

"Help!"

For Jimmy!
—N.W.

& JONAS PUBLISHING

IDW

PRESENT:

WORTHWHILE
B O O K S

www.WorthwhileChildrensBooks.com

ISBN: 978-1-60010-303-2

11 10 09 08   1 2 3 4 5

Text and illustrations copyright © 2008 Nick Ward.

Published by arrangement with Meadowside Children's Books, 185 Fleet Street, London EC4A 2HS.

Worthwhile Books, a division of Idea and Design Works, LLC. Editorial offices: 5080 Santa Fe Street, San Diego, CA 92109.
Any similarities to persons living or dead are purely coincidental. Printed in Korea.
Worthwhile Books does not read or accept unsolicited submissions of ideas, stories, or artwork.

Jonas Publishing, Publisher: Howard Jonas
IDW, Chairman: Morris Berger • IDW, President: Ted Adams • IDW, Senior Graphic Artist: Robbie Robbins
Worthwhile Books, Vice President and Creative Director: Rob Kurtz • Worthwhile Books, Senior Editor: Megan Bryant